THE W   RIES
FOR 5+ YEAR OLDS

Also in this series

The Walker Book of Animal Stories
The Walker Book of Funny Stories
The Walker Book of Magical Stories
The Walker Book of Stories for 6+ Year Olds

This collection first published 1995 as
A Walker Treasury: Stories for Five-Year-Olds by Walker Books Ltd
87 Vauxhall Walk, London SE11 5HJ

This edition published 2000

2 4 6 8 10 9 7 5 3 1

Text © year of publication individual authors
Illustrations © year of publication individual illustrators
Cover illustration © 2000 Tony Ross

This book has been typeset in ITC Garamond.

Printed and bound in Great Britain
by The Guernsey Press Co. Ltd

British Library Cataloguing in Publication Data
A catalogue record for this book is
available from the British Library.

ISBN 0-7445-7768-3

The Walker Book of
stories
for 5+ year olds

WALKER BOOKS
AND SUBSIDIARIES
LONDON • BOSTON • SYDNEY

CONTENTS

CLEVER CAKES
7
by Michael Rosen
illustrated by Caroline Holden

THE STORY OF QUEENIE AND TREACLE
15
by Susan Hill
illustrated by Paul Howard

ANGELS ON ROLLER-SKATES
33
written and illustrated by Maggie Harrison

THE APPLE CHILD
43
by Vivian French
illustrated by Chris Fisher

TOOTHACHE
69
by Marjorie Darke
illustrated by Shelagh McNicholas

ANDREW McANDREW AND THE GRANDFATHER CLOCK
75
by Bernard Mac Laverty
illustrated by Duncan Smith

ZENOBIA AND THE WILD LIFES
81
by Vivian French
illustrated by Duncan Smith

MARY MARY
91
by Sarah Hayes
illustrated by Helen Craig

CARRIE CLIMBS A MOUNTAIN
101
by June Crebbin
illustrated by Thelma Lambert

TOD AND THE BIRTHDAY PRESENT
115
by Philippa Pearce
illustrated by Adriano Gon

ONE VERY SMALL FOOT
129
by Dick King-Smith
illustrated by David Parkins

CLEVER CAKES

by MICHAEL ROSEN
illustrated by CAROLINE HOLDEN

Once there was a girl called Masha, who lived with her granny at the edge of the woods.

One day Masha said, "Granny, can I play outside with my friends?"

"Yes, Masha," said Granny, "but don't wander off into the woods, will you? There are dangerous animals there that bite…"

Off went Masha to play with her friends. They played hide-and-seek.

Masha went away to hide and she hid right deep in the woods. Then she waited for her friends to find her.

She waited and waited but they never came.

So Masha came out of her hiding-place and started to walk home.

She walked this way, then that way, but very soon she knew she was lost.

"He-e-e-lp!" she shouted. "He-e-e-e-lp!"

But no one came.

Then, very suddenly, up came a massive muscly bear.

"Ah hah!" said the bear. "You come with me, little girl. I'm taking you home. I want you to cook my dinner, wash my trousers and scrub the floor in my house."

"I don't want to do that or anything like it, thank you very much," said Masha. "I want to go home."

"Oh, no you don't," said the bear. "You're coming home with me." And he picked up Masha in his massive muscly paws and took her off to his house.

So now Masha had to cook and clean and wash and dust all day long. And she hated it. And she hated the massive muscly bear.

So she made a plan.

She cooked some cakes, and then she said to the bear, "Mr Bear, do you think I could take some cakes to my granny?"

I'm not falling for a stupid trick like that, thought the bear. If I let her go to her granny's, she'll never come back.

"No, you can't," he said. "I'll take your cakes to her myself."

8

And he thought, I'll eat all those cakes. Yum, yum, and yum again.

"Right," said Masha, "I'll put the cakes in this basket. Don't eat them on the way to Granny's, will you? 'Cos if you do, something terrible will happen to you."

"Of course I won't eat the cakes," said the bear.

As soon as the bear's back was turned, Masha jumped into the basket. When he turned round, he picked up the basket and walked off.

After a while, the bear got tired – ooh, that basket was so heavy, it was pulling off his arm – so he sat down.

"Now for the cakes," he said.

But Masha called out from inside the basket, "Don't you eat us, Mr Bear. We're little cakes for Masha's granny."

You should have seen that bear jump!

"The cakes heard me. Oh, yes, Masha did say if I ate them something terrible would happen to me. I'd better leave them alone."

So up got the bear and walked on …

and on …

and on …

until he began to feel hungry.

He thought, If I can eat the cakes without them knowing, surely nothing terrible will happen to me. But how can I eat them without them knowing?

Then he said out loud, "Oooh, I wonder if those little cakes would like to hop out of the basket and come for a walk with me."

But Masha called out from inside the basket, "Don't you dare touch us, you great greedy glut. We're little cakes for Masha's granny."

The bear nearly jumped out of his jacket.

"Woo-hoo, those devilish little cakes knew that was a trick. What clever cakes. Next time I won't say anything at all. I'll just sit down and gobble them up. Yum, yum, and yum again."

So up he got and walked on ...

and on ...

and on ...

but now the bear was getting really very, very hungry. It felt like there was a huge hole in his belly.

This time he remembered not to speak.

Very carefully he sat down, and slo-o-o-o-wly he reached out his massive muscly paw for the basket.

But Masha, peeking through the holes in the basket, could see what the bear was up to and she called out, "Don't you dare touch us, you horrible great greedy glut. We're little cakes for Masha's granny and if you touch us, we'll jump out of the basket faster than you can blink, and we'll eat you up, ears and all."

"Zoo-wow, those cakes must be magic!" said the bear. "I'd be crazy to touch them. I'd better take them to Masha's granny as quickly as I can or something terrible will happen to me." And he hurried on to Granny's house.

When he got there he shouted, "Open the door, Granny!"

Granny came to the door and when she saw a great big bear standing there she was scared stiff.

But little Masha called out from the basket, "Look out, Bear, your time's up. Now we're going to eat you."

Bear dropped the basket, turned, and ran off shouting, "Help, help, the cakes are going to eat me, the cakes are going to eat me!"

As soon as the bear was off and away, out of the basket popped Masha.

Oh, how pleased Granny was to see her, and how pleased Masha was to see her granny!

They hugged and kissed each other so many times that there were no kisses left till the next day.

"What a clever girl you are, to trick that big bear," said Granny.

"Never mind that," said Masha. "Let's get these cakes inside us."

And that's what they did.

Yum …

     yum …

         and yum again!

THE STORY OF QUEENIE AND TREACLE

by SUSAN HILL
illustrated by PAUL HOWARD

One fine Saturday morning, Lucy Billings heard someone calling and calling in the garden of the house next door. At first it was just one voice but after a few minutes there were two. So she ran upstairs to her bedroom and looked out of the window, and from there, she could see Jane Jones and her mother going up and down their garden and they were both calling and calling. Only Lucy couldn't hear exactly *what* they were calling and she very much wanted to know. So she ran downstairs again and out of the back door and all the way up to the end of the garden of Beehive Cottage, to where there was an open bit of fence. She climbed up on the fence and looked over the top and then she could see *and* hear.

Jane Jones and her mother were looking under the hedge and beside the hedge and in the sheds, and as they looked they both called, "Queenie!

15

Queenie!" over and over again.

Lucy knew quite well who Queenie was. A week ago, when Jane Jones and her mother and father and brother Jack had moved into the house next door, Queenie had come too, in a wicker basket with a lid. When Lucy had gone round with her mother to take a tray of tea and cakes for them all, because the electricity at Old Leas Farmhouse wasn't working yet, the basket had been in the middle of the kitchen floor, and it had been making a frightful noise, a sort of squealy-mewly-yeowly sort of noise. And when Lucy had bent down and lifted up a corner of the basket, there had been two green eyes and one brown and one black pointed ear, and a pair of white whiskers.

Later, when all the doors were closed, Mrs Jones had let them open the lid of the wicker basket right up and there had been Queenie. She was a very pretty, very dainty, very small cat, and she looked as if someone had taken a brush full of brown paint and a brush full of orange paint and a brush full of black, and painted a bit of each here and there, just as the fancy took them, and then added a dab of white for luck.

"Not a proper tortoiseshell cat, I'm afraid," Mrs Jones had said.

"Not a proper anything," Jane Jones had said.

"In fact, a bit of a mess really," Mr Jones had said.

But then they had *all* said that they loved her just the same, and that was why they were being very careful only to let her out of the basket when all the doors were closed. Because Old Leas Farmhouse would be very strange indeed to Queenie, it would look strange and feel strange and most of all, it would smell strange, and she would be very puzzled and very frightened until she got quite used to living there and had learned her way about properly.

"If we open the door now, and Queenie gets out, she'll just try to run back to our old house, and that's such a long way away that she'd be lost almost at once," said Mrs Jones.

So they had stroked and petted Queenie and then let her explore the kitchen. She had got out of the basket and sniffed and looked and sniffed and crept, twitching her whiskers and waving her tail, and occasionally just sitting down and yeowling a great, sad yeowl. After a while, Mrs Jones had put her back in the basket and closed the lid, and the basket had creaked and heaved about for a minute and then gone quite quiet and still.

"She's asleep," said Jane Jones.

* * *

So when Lucy stood on the open bit of fence and saw Jane and her mother going up and down, and heard them calling and calling, she guessed at once what had happened.

"Did Queenie get out?" she shouted to them. "Have you lost her?"

And Jane Jones said yes, they had. "And she's been lost since last night and we've called and called her and put out a dish of milk and we can't find her anywhere and perhaps she'll be lost for ever and ever," she said, and then she began to cry, so that Lucy thought she must certainly not stand there on the fence but go and help look for Queenie straight away.

"I'm going to ask if I can come," she shouted to Jane Jones and quickly scrambled down from the fence and ran indoors. Her mother had already said that Jane could come and play at Beehive Cottage for the morning if she would like to, and Lucy had thought all over again how very nice it was to have a friend-next-door.

So she rushed into the kitchen and said, "Jane Jones has lost Queenie – they opened the door and she got out and they're calling and calling but they can't find her anywhere and please may I go and help them look?"

"Yes, I heard them calling," her mother said. "Oh dear. Wait a minute and I'll come with you. But first we should really see if she's got through the hedge into our garden and is hiding anywhere here."

Then Lucy's mother picked up Rosie, the baby, out of her playpen, where she had been piling up plastic bricks and knocking them down again, and they all went outside and joined in the search.

They searched under the hedge bottom on their side all the way round the garden, and inside the tool shed and the wood store and the garage and the loft above the garage. They called and called and called, and in the garden of the house next door, Jane Jones and her mother went on searching and calling. And in the middle of it all, Lucy heard the whiny noise of Frank's milk float, so she ran down the drive to the front gate, where Frank was just taking out the five bottles of milk to put in their box.

"Hello, jam-pot, how are you today?"

Frank the milkman always had a different name for Lucy, and a lot of names were very silly; they were names like "lettuce leaf" and "teacup" and "cough drop", and they made Lucy laugh. But today she didn't laugh, she said at once, "Jane Jones has lost her cat Queenie – they left a door open and she got out and

they've searched and searched and called and called and so have we but we can't find her anywhere."

And Frank said, "Dear me, I don't like to hear that. You tell me what this little Queenie-cat looks like, and I'll keep my eye open. She won't have gone far."

"She's brown and orange and black, all mixed up with some white bits, and Mrs Jones says she might try to go back to where they lived before and that's a very long way away."

"No, no, she'll be used to the new smells by now, and she'll know this is where she lives because her people are here, you see, and all the chairs and tables and rugs as well." And Frank banged the gate shut and climbed back into his milk float with a cheerful smile.

"I'll keep an eye open. We'll find little Queenie-cat, she won't be far away." And he winked at Lucy and off went the milk float, whiny-whiny-rattle-chink up the lane.

But Lucy wasn't sure, and a bit later, when Jane Jones and her mother came into Beehive Cottage, *they* weren't sure either, and Jane said she thought Queenie was lost for ever, and began to cry again.

"Come upstairs and play, and I'll let you dress and undress Violet, if you like," said Lucy. Violet was her last-birthday doll, and still very special. So she and

Jane Jones went upstairs and played with Violet, and after that, they did each other's hair and used Lucy's mother's slides and grips and hair combs to make themselves into grown-up ladies, and they almost – but not quite – forgot about Queenie, and Jane didn't cry any more. Only once she said, in the middle of pulling off Violet's petticoat, "But she wouldn't have come to your house because of Jessie. She's frightened of dogs." Jessie was the Billings family's big black labrador.

"Well, Frank the milkman said he'd look out for her, and tell everybody, and he said she wouldn't have got far."

"Oh," said Jane. But she didn't look very happy.

That afternoon, they all went in Mrs Jones' car to the park in Stillford, where there was a playground with slides and swings and a rope-walk and a roundabout, and a pond with ducks. Afterwards, they walked under the chestnut trees collecting conkers in two carrier bags. Rosie and Jack got out of their pushchairs and ran about and tried to find conkers too, but usually they brought back handfuls of leaves and a few stones instead. The sun was shining and they all got quite warm and piled their coats into the pushchairs and then ran about a lot more, before going to the café in the park, where they sat at tables outside on the grass. They had orange squash and scones and jam and chocolate biscuits, and it was only when she was finishing her second biscuit that Jane Jones suddenly said, "But if she's lost for ever, who will give Queenie anything to eat?" and burst out crying all over again. Her mother hugged her and said of course they would find Queenie in the end, they'd go home now, at once, and carry on searching.

"And Daddy will look."

"And *my* daddy will," said Lucy.

"Yes," said Jane, "and all the daddies in Codling Village."

And so they did. Or at least, a great many of them, and a lot of other people besides, because Frank the milkman had been round and asked them to. And Jane Jones' mother wrote out two notices on postcards. They read:

LOST

QUEENIE, OUR SMALL BROWN,
ORANGE AND BLACK CAT WITH
WHITE WHISKERS. IF FOUND,
PLEASE RETURN TO
OLD LEAS FARMHOUSE.

Then they walked up to Mrs Dobby's post office shop, and she kindly said she would put one of the notices in her window, and they pinned the other one on the village notice board by the telephone box. "There," said Mrs Jones, "now Queenie is sure to be found."

But she wasn't. Not that day or the next or the next, even though Lucy's father and Jane Jones' father went all the way down Magpie Lane to the fields and even as far as the wood, searching in the hedges and ditches with sticks, and Mr Day at Codling Farm let them go into his barns and hayrick and stables and cowsheds and outhouses to look, too. They said they had seen just about every other kind of cat there, because Mr Day had so many farm cats he'd lost count. But not Queenie.

On the fourth day, which was Wednesday, the most astonishing thing happened. Lucy and Jane Jones had come back from the playgroup, and they were playing in the outside yard of Old Leas Farmhouse with a lot of cardboard boxes and packing cases which had been used to bring all the Jones' things when they had moved, and which Mr Jones hadn't got round to breaking up or burning yet. They hoped very much that he wouldn't, because the boxes made excellent houses and railway carriages and tea tables. And in the middle of playing, Jane Jones happened to look round, and said, "Oh look, oh look! It's Queenie. Queenie's come home!"

Lucy looked, and there, walking daintily down the garden, came the little brown and orange and black cat, Queenie. And she was carrying something very carefully in her mouth.

"What has she got?" Jane Jones shouted. "Oh, whatever has Queenie got?"

Just then, Mrs Jones came out of the back door holding Jack, and they all looked as Queenie walked towards them.

She came right up to where they stood and then she stopped in front of Jane.

"It's a kitten!" Jane Jones said.

And so it was. A small browny-yellowy coloured kitten. Queenie set it down very gently on the cobbles and gave a loud meowl, and the kitten looked up at them all and gave a meowl that was almost as loud.

"Is it *her* kitten?" Lucy asked.

"Oh no, it can't be," Mrs Jones said, and she bent down and stroked the kitten's head. "It's quite big – two or three weeks old, anyway, and we've only been here a week and Queenie certainly didn't have a kitten when we came."

"Then whose is it? Where did she get it from?" asked Jane and Lucy together.

But of course Mrs Jones didn't know. Nor did anybody else, though they asked all about Codling Village, and even put up another two notices saying:

FOUND

ONE BROWNY-YELLOW KITTEN.

PLEASE CLAIM FROM

OLD LEAS FARMHOUSE.

But nobody did claim him and nobody had any idea whose kitten it was either, and where Queenie had gone to for those four days was a mystery, too.

"I told you she wouldn't have gone far away," said Frank the milkman, when he heard. Only Lucy thought that she might have been, she might have been miles and miles and miles. But nobody would ever be able to find out.

Mrs Dobby at the post office shop was very glad to hear that Queenie had come home, but she wasn't a bit surprised. "That's cats for you," she said, "they just turn up when they feel like it."

But the oddest thing of all was that although Queenie had brought the kitten back in her mouth, and they seemed to be very happy together, what the kitten liked best was following Lucy Billings home to Beehive Cottage, and sometimes even to come to look for her when she was already there without Jane Jones. However often they took it back to the house next door, sooner or later it would just turn up again, so that in the end, Lucy's father said they might just as well give in and keep it. Only Lucy's mother said she wasn't so sure about that, they had quite enough mouths to feed as it was.

But one cold morning, they came downstairs into the kitchen to find the kitten curled up with Jessie in her basket by the range, and after that, Lucy's mother said it looked as if the kitten had got its feet under the table. Which Lucy thought was a very odd thing to say.

Then her father asked Lucy what she wanted to call the kitten and said, "I think Turn-up would be about right, myself," but Lucy said you couldn't call a cat Turn-up.

"I shall call it Treacle," she said, "because it looks like that."

After that, Treacle usually slept in Jessie's basket, curled up together with Jessie. Only sometimes, for no particular reason, it went off and lived at the house next door for a day or two. But it always came back, and after a while, Queenie even came with it occasionally and wasn't frightened of Jessie any

more, though she would never actually get right into the basket, like Treacle.

"They're a bit like you two, those cats," Jane Jones' mother said one afternoon to Jane and Lucy, "living in each other's houses half the time!" Which was perfectly true!

ANGELS ON ROLLER-SKATES

written and illustrated by
MAGGIE HARRISON

Bigun was big for his age and proud of it.

Middlun was smaller, but she had an extra long plait to make up for it.

Littlun was smallest of all. He got in everybody's way when he was crawling and got on everyone's nerves when he was yelling.

One day Middlun discovered how to draw angels. She drew a person first, and then she drew a tall triangle on each shoulder.

She was amazed. All her people now had wings, and all of them were angels. She drew and drew and drew.

When she ran out of paper she drew on the fridge door. Mum wasn't pleased, because that sort of red felt-tip doesn't come off properly and it left pink ghost angels all over the white enamel.

Then Middlun discovered that if she drew crisscross lines on her people's feet and two little circles underneath each foot, then all her people were wearing roller-skates. She was ecstatic. Now all her angels were on roller-skates! She drew them skating over hills and skating across bridges. She drew them skating up steps.

Bigun was scornful.

"You can't roller-skate *down* steps, you idiot."

"They're roller-skating *up* steps, Bigun. Can't you tell up from down?"

"It doesn't matter. You can't roller-skate up *or* down steps."

"Angels can," said Middlun. "That's the difference between us and them."

Mum was becoming frazzled by it all, but then Dad gave Middlun a whole roll of wallpaper so she could draw on the back of it.

Middlun was almost delirious with joy. She rolled it along the landing floor, and drew and drew and drew.

Angels with roller-skates were riding on horses. Angels with roller-skates were sitting on roof tops having a rest. Angels with roller-skates were having a wonderful picnic on the beach, with a huge tablecloth spread out on the sand, and all Middlun's favourite food was drawn on little plates. There were chocolate biscuits and banana sandwiches, a small piece of roast lamb in a great green sea of mint jelly, pink milk shakes and waffles, asparagus soup and cheese slices, and a very large dish of prawn cocktail.

Bigun sat on the banisters and watched.

"I told you you were an idiot. If you roller-skated on the beach you'd get sand in the ball-bearings. Then they wouldn't work at all."

"Bigun," Mum shouted from the kitchen, "why don't you stop being so critical? In any case, I don't think skates even have ball-bearings these days."

"Well, mine do. Those ones you got me from Oxfam with the special little spanner to make them bigger. They keep leaking ball-bearings all over the pavement. I'm always trying to scoop them up and pour them back."

Mum decided it was time to change the subject before Bigun suggested he needed a new pair, with brakes and four-wheel drive. She knew how much *they* cost.

"Middlun, would you stop drawing now, because it's very nearly suppertime and I want to wash your hair afterwards. Don't you remember what's happening tomorrow?"

Middlun finished drawing an enormous hot cross bun, big enough for all the angels at the picnic to share, and reluctantly began to roll up the paper.

"Yes, I'm going to school." She looked at Bigun, hoping that he would fall off the banisters in surprise. Or at least look impressed. He did neither.

"How boring," was all he said and he wandered off to watch the weather forecast until supper was ready.

Middlun was starting school properly next term, but all the new children had been invited to school for a morning, to meet the teachers and find out what they would be doing in the reception class. A parent had to come too, in case.

"In case what?" Middlun asked.

"In case you're scared. Of a new place, or lots of big children. Anything," said Mum.

But Middlun was not scared. She was looking forward to it.

It was Mum who was nervous. And Bigun. He was always a bit of a worrier.

"You don't go in our door, Mum, you use the green one round the side. And Mrs Mitchell's got shaggy hair and green glasses. You can't miss her. Can Middlun read her own name, 'cos she'll have to, to find her peg? They don't use pictures except in the nursery. And are all her clothes named, or she'll lose them sure as anything? Mrs Mitchell gets ratty if clothes aren't named."

"For goodness' sake, Bigun, that's why we're going tomorrow. In any case, it's not so long ago that

I was taking *you* for the first time, remember? I don't suppose everything has changed since then. Stop worrying Middlun."

But Middlun wasn't in the least worried. She was remembering not to forget to draw some lemon cheesecake for the angels' picnic on the beach. She thought angels would like it.

Mum and Middlun arrived at school the next morning and remembered to use the side door.

Mrs Mitchell sat all the new children round an orange table and gave them scissors and paste and lots of magazines to cut up and make into sticky pictures. Then she talked quietly to the parents.

The children at all the other tables were being very good. But while their hands were busy doing things, their eyes were watching the new ones. The little boy next to Middlun couldn't make his scissors work, so he started crying. His dad dropped the information sheets Mrs Mitchell was giving him and rushed to pick him up.

Middlun looked round the room with interest. One group was coiling pots out of Plasticine snakes. Mum wouldn't let her have Plasticine at home because Bigun had squidged some into the carpet.

Middlun picked up her chair and squeezed herself in at the coiled pot table.

"Hello, friends," she said cheerfully, "can I play?" She took a chunk of purple Plasticine from a little girl with pale hair and started rolling a long snake. The little girl decided that she didn't want purple anyway, and took some green to make a handle for her pot.

Mum knew it was time to go. Middlun was happy, but if there was going to be a rumpus about her being on the wrong table, Mum was sure Mrs Mitchell would handle it better if she wasn't there.

"See you later then." She waved as she went out, but Middlun wasn't looking. Her snake now stretched almost to the end of the table and the little girl with pale hair was showing her how to make a pot with it.

When Mum came back at lunch time to collect her, all the other children were clutching sticky pictures, and windmills made out of loo rolls and wooden lolly sticks. Middlun had nothing to take home. Mrs Mitchell explained: "The big table were doing a poster competition for the Children's Hospital. The best picture from this area will be sent up to London and win a prize. Middlun really wanted to do one too, after she had finished her Plasticine. I couldn't stop her. I suppose it's all right to send it in with the others because by the time they do the judging she will be a member of the school."

Mum laughed. "Please don't worry about sending it in. I'm sure Middlun won't mind."

Middlun glared at her.

"I will. It's a very good picture." Before Mum had time to say anything, Mrs Mitchell sent Middlun off to find her coat and whispered, "It *is* amazingly good. Most original. They were supposed to do something about hospitals, and most of them, of course, painted pictures of children with spots, or sitting up in bed all bandaged up. Your daughter painted a nurse with angel's wings. And do you know, the nurse was on roller-skates! Now isn't that unusual? I think it stands a very good chance."

When they got home, Mum told Dad and Bigun all about Middlun's introduction to school, and the poster competition.

"I suppose Middlun did an angel on roller-skates?" Dad sighed.

"Of course I did," said Middlun. "Only I put her in a blue striped dress with a white cap and apron and a big red cross on the cap to show she was a nurse. And I put in one of those little upside-down watches they wear on their aprons too."

"What's the prize?" asked Bigun. But they had forgotten to ask.

A few weeks later they found out Middlun had won the prize, and her picture was going to be used as a huge poster all over the area. She was invited to the Children's Hospital with her family and Mrs Mitchell for the presentation. Cameras clicked and everybody clapped while she opened the box. Only Mrs Mitchell guessed what might be in it. And she was right. Inside was a brand new pair of the most beautiful roller-skates you've ever seen.

THE
APPLE CHILD

by VIVIAN FRENCH
illustrated by CHRIS FISHER

There was once a cold village on the side of a tall cold mountain. Behind the village was a stony field where a flock of thin sheep huddled together under the shadow of a few spindly apple trees, and high above the mountain hung the moon; a pale cold moon that sent long dark shadows sprawling along the ground, creeping in and out of the village, and crouching down beside Ben's small cold cottage.

"Brrrr," shivered Ben, pulling an old sack round his shoulders. A little fire flickered in the grate, but there was no more wood left in the broken basket by the chimney. He got up and stared out of the window. Up on the mountainside he could see the apple trees quivering in the wind.

"I'll run up and see if there are any twigs or sticks under the trees," said Ben. He wrapped the sack more closely about himself, and slipped out of the cottage and up the street. The wind caught him and tugged and pulled at him, but he put his head down and trudged on to where the cold field lay beyond the last house.

The sheep shifted unwillingly as Ben walked among them; "Saaaad," they bleated, "saaad!" The trees were moaning and muttering to each other, the wind snapped at their branches and whipped their last few leaves off and away. High in the sky the moon gazed down. Ben glanced up, and for a moment thought he saw a watching silver face.

"What can I do, Moon?" he called. "I'm cold – I'm ever so cold!"

There was no answer from the moon, but the wind suddenly dropped. Just for a moment there was a stillness, a silence as if all the moonlit world was holding its breath. Only a moment it lasted, and then up sprang the wind with a howl and a shriek, and tore the sack from his back. The trees bent and swayed, and with a loud crash a long branch fell to the ground beside him.

"Thank you! Thank you!" Ben shouted, and he picked up the branch and ran as fast as he could back to his small cold cottage. The fire was a mere glimmer but, as he fed it, first the smallest twig and then the bigger ones, it began to take heart and to glow warmly. Breaking the branch, he built the fire up higher, until the shadows were dancing and the smell of apple wood filled the room.

"Oh!" Ben stared as the flames sparkled and crackled and burnt red and green and silver.

Crack! A log of the apple wood split into two halves, and a small green child no bigger than Ben's hand stepped out of the fire and on to the floor beside him.

"Good evening," said the child.

Ben couldn't speak. He stared and stared at the little green figure, and looked into the fire, and then back again.

"If you're wondering where I come from," said the child, "I come from the apple log. I'm an apple child – how do you do, and what's your name?"

"I'm Ben," said Ben, still staring.

The apple child smiled. "Glad to meet you. And now, how about supper?"

Ben shook his head. "I'm sorry," he said, "I've nothing but a few old seed potatoes in a sack in the yard."

"Let's fetch them in," said the apple child. "There's nothing like a big baked potato."

Ben shook his head again. How could an apple child know that seed potatoes were poor shrivelled green things that could never be eaten? He went slowly out into the bitterly cold wind.

The sack was behind the door, just where the farmer had left it. The sack was there – but it wasn't nearly empty. To Ben's amazement, it was full to splitting with fine, clean, rich yellow potatoes. He chose four of the biggest and hurried back inside.

"Put them to bake on the fire," said the apple child. "I'm hungry!"

Ben slept well that night. He woke in the morning to find the sun bursting in through the window.

"Good morning," said a cheerful voice. "Shall we have eggs for our breakfast?"

Ben rubbed his eyes, and saw the apple child standing beside him holding two big brown eggs.

"That's a splendid black hen you have," said the apple child. "She's hiding a nest behind the blackberry bushes."

"But she's been gone for months," Ben said. "I was certain the fox had had her for dinner."

"Not she," said the apple child. "And I found a few good nuts on the walnut tree."

Ben looked curiously at the apple child. Had he grown in the night? It seemed to Ben that he had, although he was still the smallest child he had ever seen. And what magic was he working? Even Ben's bare cold room felt full of warmth and the smell of apple wood and sunshine and flowers.

"Well?" asked the apple child. "Have you decided? Soft- or hard-boiled eggs?"

Ben and the apple child settled down happily. It seemed to Ben that the cottage was always warm now, and full of sunlight. The black hen was laying steadily, and his two little brown and white bantams had reappeared, clucking happily, from under the hawthorn hedge. Ben was quite sure that he had, with his very own eyes, seen them both being carried off by foxes, but he smiled and collected the small brown eggs. When Mrs Wutherlop from next door came by to ask if he could spare an egg or two he was more than willing, and he took the crusty bread she offered him in exchange with pleasure.

Strong green shoots sprang up in Ben's bare back garden, and he found that he was growing the finest cabbages and leeks and carrots in the village – more than enough for him and the apple child. Ben filled

his wheelbarrow and took his extra vegetables to the shop, and came home chinking real money in his pocket, the first he had had for weeks and months and years. He didn't see old Mrs Crabbitty in the opposite cottage peering out of her window as he hopped along the road, and he didn't see Mrs Crabbitty poking and sniffing at the crisp green cabbages and creamy white leeks in the shop, her little black eyes gleaming greedily.

"Them's Ben's leeks, you says? And carrotses? Well, well, well…" and she shuffled home, mumbling to herself.

That evening Mrs Crabbitty came knocking on Ben's door.

"Seems things is a-picking up for you, young man," she said, her eyes slipping and sliding as she stared over Ben's shoulder into the glowing room beyond. "Seems as if you found yourself a liddle slip of luck."

Ben felt uncomfortable. He had never liked Mrs Crabbitty, but he knew she lived on what she could beg or borrow from the village, and had nothing of her own.

"Would you care to come in?" he asked, with a small sigh.

"There now," said Mrs Crabbitty, whisking

through the door and settling herself by the crackling flames. "There's a fine fire."

Ben looked around. He had last seen the apple child toasting his toes on the hearth, but there was no sign of him now. He felt Mrs Crabbitty's beady black eyes searching round and about, and he hastily turned back to her.

"Looking for something?" Mrs Crabbitty asked him. "Or, maybe, for someone?"

Ben shook his head.

Mrs Crabbitty brought two shining steel knitting needles out of her pocket, and a small ball of grey, greasy wool. She began to knit, and while she knitted she swayed a little and hummed a strange tuneless drone.

Ben couldn't take his eyes away from the flashing silver needles, and when Mrs Crabbitty began to ask him questions about the garden, and the little black hen, and the never-ending supply of wood in the basket, he was unable to stop himself telling her all about his visit to the moonlit orchard, and the coming of the apple child.

"So, you just threw the wood on the fire, young man?" Mrs Crabbitty asked, clicking her needles and swaying.

"Yes," Ben said, his voice creeping away from him like a small sly snake.

"Then what's good for the young will be good for us old ones," said Mrs Crabbitty. She sat up straight, and snapped the shining needles together. Hauling herself up on to her feet she nodded at Ben.

"I'll be off to my own poor place," she said. "But I'll be having a special sort of a blaze tonight, nows I knows what's what."

Ben watched her scuttle away. He was surprised to see that she didn't go straight home, but went away down the road, pulling her shawl round her shoulders.

Mrs Crabbitty scurried along towards the end of the village street.

"I'll fetch meself a slice of luck," she said, rubbing her hands together. A sharp gust of wind caught at her shawl and tossed it away in front of her until it caught on the branch of a tall tree standing at the very edge of the orchard.

"Dratted wind!" Mrs Crabbitty struggled towards the tree, and pulled at her shawl. It came with a wrench, and brought a shower of twigs and a twisted branch with it that fell at her feet.

"Well, well, well." Mrs Crabbitty bent and picked

up the branch. "Maybe here's me luck, after all." And she hurried back towards her dark and dusty house. The wind grew louder than ever, and rushed in between the apple trees with a shriek so that they shook and quivered under the moon.

Mrs Crabbitty's fire was a mere glimmer in the darkness of her dusty, spidered room, but she fed it with pieces of loose bark until an uncertain flame flickered. Then she took the entire branch, and pushed it into the back of the fireplace. First one green flame and then another sprang up, but there was no heat to be felt; the blaze was as cold as the fire at the heart of a bitter green emerald.

"Now, I'd like company, so's all me work gets done for me. No reason why lazy boys should have all the luck."

Mrs Crabbitty peered into the grate, and the branch began to twist. There was a splitting and a splintering, and something shapeless came slithering out on to the hearth. It squirmed itself into a long-bodied, bandy-legged, large-headed creature, and then it began to grow. Mrs Crabbitty, watching open-mouthed, saw it bulge and stretch and twist until it was pressed up against her cracked and yellowed ceiling. Only then did it stop growing.

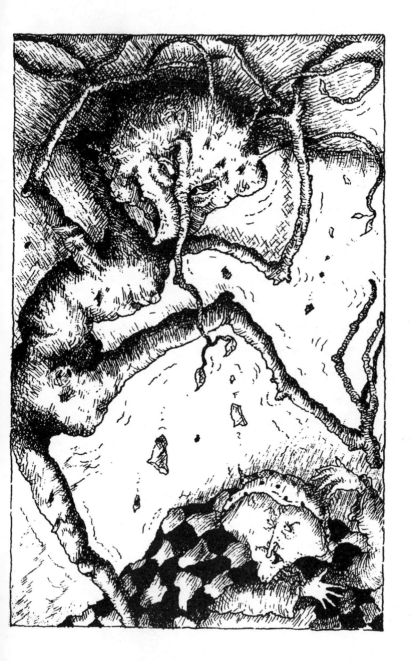

Mrs Crabbitty reached behind her for her chair, and sat down with a flump. The creature turned and looked at her with its glassy eyes, and she stared back.

"What kind of a thing ezactly are you?"

"Elder Bogle," growled the creature in a voice that was full of gravel and grit.

"Ah," said Mrs Crabbitty. "And why ain't you an apple child to help a poor woman?"

"Elder branch." The bogle pointed a bent and wrinkled finger at the smouldering fire.

"Is that so? And what ezactly can you do?"

A movement on the table caught Mrs Crabbitty's eye, and turning, she saw a bowl of small apples blackening and rotting as she watched. The elder bogle watched as well, and as the last apple shrank into nothingness he smiled a sour and twisted smile.

Mrs Crabbitty sucked her lower lip thoughtfully.

"If you and I is to live together," she said, "I'll thank you to leave *my* goodies alone."

The elder bogle gave her a cold look, but it said nothing. It folded itself up into a dark heap, and appeared to go to sleep.

Mrs Crabbitty took her shawl and climbed up to

bed. Before she went to sleep she thought for a long time and then, smiling, closed her eyes.

Ben and the apple child heard about the elder bogle from Mrs Wutherlop. She came knocking on the cottage door the next morning, carrying a jug of sour milk and a dish of moulded and pitted plums.

"What is it?" Ben asked. "What's happened?"

Mrs Wutherlop began to cry. "Mrs Crabbitty," she sobbed, "her said that if I don't give her milk each day she'd witch me. And I says no, an' she whistles up a horrible bogle thing, an' now there's nothing fit to eat in my larder, nor yet a green leaf in my garden, an' the kitten's crying its heart out. And it's the same to all the folks in the village who won't do what she says, up comes that there bogle, an' the milk turns sour an' the hens don't lay an' the pigsies are as thin as a rail. And us doesn't know what to do!" Mrs Wutherlop sat down on Ben's step and threw her apron over her head.

Ben patted Mrs Wutherlop's shoulder, but she went on crying. He hurried out to his own garden, but there everything was growing and green. He peeped over the fence, and at once saw the terrible bareness where Mrs Wutherlop's carrots and onions and potatoes had been. Even the holly tree was as bare as a winter's oak.

Ben picked up a basket and filled it with walnuts and eggs and apples and cabbages from his larder, and put it down beside the still sobbing Mrs Wutherlop. Then he went to see if the apple child knew what might be happening.

The apple child was, as usual, sitting and feeding the fire with twigs and sticks.

"There's something terrible come to the village!" Ben said. The apple child nodded. "Mrs Crabbitty's slice of luck."

Ben squatted down by the child. "Is there anything we can do?" he asked. "Can you make Mrs Wutherlop's garden grow again like you made mine?"

The apple child stood up and stretched. "There's not room for an elder bogle and an apple child in the one village," he said.

"What do you mean?" Ben asked anxiously. "You don't mean you're going to go away?"

The apple child smiled. "We'll see," he said. "Elder bogles are strong, but they're not always clever."

"I'll come with you," said Ben, as the apple child moved towards the door. "I'm not scared – well, not very."

* * *

Ben and the apple child walked out of the cottage and past Mrs Wutherlop.

She had stopped crying, and was holding the basket of vegetables closely to herself as if they were protection. When she saw Ben and the apple child going across to Mrs Crabbitty's cottage she followed them.

Mrs Crabbitty was sitting on a bench at the side of her cracked and crumbling cottage.

She was shelling a bowl of fresh peas, and six or seven fine fat hens were clucking and fussing about her feet.

Piled up against her cottage wall were strings of onions, jugs of thick golden cream, sweet cured hams, pies and pastries with shining sugar crusts, russet apples and a huge grass twist of strawberries.

There was no sign of the elder bogle.

Mrs Crabbitty looked up and saw Ben and the apple child. Her face looked pinched and sour and as if she too was growing moulded and rotten.

"And what would you be after?" Her voice sounded thinner and sharper. "These things is all mine, mind you. Mrs Crabbitty's found her luck."

Ben didn't know what to say. The apple child was saying nothing at all. He was looking up at the little

windows of the cottage where a dark shadow was moving behind the dust and the cobwebs. There was a slithering and a sliding, and the doorway was filled with the twisted shape of the elder bogle. When it saw the apple child it began to hiss, and its eyes glowed greedily.

"Now, my pet," said Mrs Crabbitty, "what's troubling you?"

The elder bogle cracked its bony knuckles and stretched out its skinny arm towards the apple child.

"Go away," it growled. It waved at the house behind it, and the village in front. *Mine! All mine!*

The apple child still said nothing, but he shook his head. The elder bogle began to snarl.

"Fight!" Its teeth were long and yellow, and Ben took a step backwards. He was glad to find Mrs Wutherlop close behind him, and she put a large freckled hand on his shoulder.

"Fight!" The elder bogle was circling round the apple child, growling and sniffing and snarling.

"Wait." The child's voice was small but very clear. "I won't fight, but I challenge you: a test – a test of strength."

The elder bogle and Mrs Crabbitty both laughed a sour, cackling laugh, and then the elder bogle nodded its heavy head. It turned round and round until it saw the tall old pine tree that sheltered Mrs Crabbitty's cottage. Crouching down, it clasped its long arms about the tree's huge trunk, and then with a grunt and a heave it wrenched the quivering tree out of the ground. With a gravelly snarl it stood up, the pine on its shoulder, and began to make its way up the mountain towards a wind-blasted tree at the very top.

Mrs Crabbitty gave a shrill scream of laughter. "There, my fine friends. He can carry the tallest tree on his shoulder, all the way up to the top and all the way down. A test of strength, you says – I says the same – can you do as well? Look, see, already he's at the top!"

Ben watched in horror. Even with the massive pine tree on his back the elder bogle was leaping and jumping across the rough mountainside. The apple child was as light as the wind, how could he possibly carry any such load?

The apple child seemed unconcerned. He was choosing an apple from Mrs Wutherlop's basket, and when he had carefully chosen one he polished it on his sleeve.

"Huzzah! Huzzah! Here comes my pet, my pretty poppet!" Mrs Crabbitty waved her bony arms in the air as the elder bogle came loping back down the

village street. It was still carrying the pine tree on one shoulder, and on the other shoulder was a massive branch from the stricken tree on the top of the mountain. With a snarl of victory it slid to a stop in front of Mrs Crabbitty, and tossed the huge pine tree right over her cottage. Ben felt the ground shudder under his feet, and a trembling in the air as the old pine crashed to the earth.

"You!" shouted the elder bogle, sneering down at the apple child.

The apple child nodded. He touched Ben with his hand, and sprang away up the street towards the mountain. He ran as if he was dancing, and the apple trees fluttered and rustled as he passed them. He ran as if he was flying, and the birds overhead swooped lower and circled above his head. He spun three times round the tree at the very top of the mountain, and then ran back to the village with the ease of a stream flowing over a grassy bank. He touched Ben once again, and the time that he had taken was less than half that taken by the elder bogle.

"I say the apple child wins!" called out Ben, but his voice was uncertain. The elder bogle and Mrs Crabbitty snorted, and the elder bogle stamped its leathery foot so hard that a grey dust flew up, making Ben cough and rub his eyes.

"You called for a test of strength," said Mrs Crabbitty, shaking her fist. "And I says as my pretty pet is the winner!"

The elder bogle grinned a wicked yellow-toothed grin, and rubbed its gnarled and withered hands together. Mrs Crabbitty pointed at Ben. "You and yours have had your chances. So, be off with you!"

Ben's shoulders drooped, and he nodded hopelessly. "We'll go," he said, and turned away.

"Just one moment."

The apple child was standing in front of them. In his hand was an apple, and as they all stared at him he broke it in half, and showed it to the elder bogle.

"Six pips," he said. "Six seeds – *so*! You carried *one* tree, but I carried *six* apple trees up and round the mountain ... six tiny living trees in one apple. I am the winner, and I claim the village for my own."

The elder bogle let out a shriek that made Ben clutch his ears. Mrs Crabbitty screamed, a high piercing scream.

"Tricksied! We've been tricksied!"

The elder bogle howled and wailed and stamped his foot. The earth beneath Ben's feet shook, and a swirl of grey-green dust flew up into the air. The elder bogle stamped again, and the ground split beneath him.

"No! My poppitty! My pet!" Mrs Crabbitty sank on

to her knees, but the elder bogle was already gone. All that was left was a clump of green leaves.

"Oh! Oh! Oh!" said Mrs Crabbitty, and she scuttled into her cottage like a frightened spider.

The apple child looked after her. "She'll do no harm now," he said.

Mrs Wutherlop took Ben's arm.

"A nice cup of tea wouldn't come amiss. Eh, what a carry on!"

Ben turned to the apple child. "Is it all over? Should we go home?"

"Yes," said the apple child. "Hurry on home."

Something in his voice made Ben stare at him. "Aren't you coming too?"

The apple child shook his head. "I'll be about," he said. "Here and there…"

Ben sighed. "I shall miss you," he said.

Mrs Wutherlop patted Ben's shoulder. "You can come and sit with me for company," she said. "And I've a kitten that's looking for a home."

The apple child waved, and moved towards the apple trees on the mountainside.

They were heavy with ripe red apples, and the sheep grazing beneath were fat and thickly fleeced.

Even the bare mountainside was flushed with patches of soft green grass and clusters of bushes.

"Goodbye, Ben," said the apple child.

"Goodbye," said Ben, "and thank you." He could feel tears at the back of his eyes, and there was a lump in his throat. Turning, he ran after the warm and comfortable figure of Mrs Wutherlop. The apple child paused for a moment, and then slipped in among the apple trees.

On the edge of the deepening blue sky a golden harvest moon was rising and, high above, a single star watched over the village. Shadows stretched out from the richly laden trees, like thick ribbons of warm black velvet binding the small houses and cottages safely together, and the moon smiled as it sailed on over the mountain.

TOOTHACHE

by MARJORIE DARKE
illustrated by SHELAGH McNICHOLAS

"We'll go to the dentist tomorrow," Dad said.

"Why?" asked Emma. She was cutting paper shapes.

"So he can look at our teeth."

"I'll go another day," Emma said. "I'm busy tomorrow."

Dad started to wash up. "The dentist is busy every day. He's made a special time to see us tomorrow. It wouldn't be friendly if we didn't turn up. Think about it."

Emma thought about it while she cut paper shapes. Then forgot about it while she rode her trike, played ball, went to the shops with Dad, ate her tea, put on her pyjamas, had a bedtime story.

After the story she went upstairs to bed.

"Don't forget to clean your teeth," Dad called.

But she did forget, because on the way she stopped to say goodnight to a spider who lived on the top stair. He had lived there a long time, but tonight he had gone.

"He's gone to see his gran," Emma said. "Then he had an ice-cream. Then he felt sick. Then he went to hospital." She went into her room. "Then the nurse put him to bed." She climbed into her bed. "Then he had … some … medicine…" Then she went to sleep.

In the middle of the night something woke her up. For a minute she thought of going to find Dad, when…

"URRRRRRG!" the something said. "OWOWOWEEEEEEK!"

Emma smiled. She hung over the side of her bed.

Underneath, two big shiny red eyes looked back at her. Tears spouted down two little crinkly cheeks, dripped off a wobbly chin and fell on two furry feet.

Her friend the monster, who lived under the bed!

"Whatever's the matter?" Emma asked.

The monster opened his wide mouth and she saw two rows of very green teeth.

"You've got toothache!" she said. "What did I tell you about remembering to clean your teeth?"

The monster hung his head.

71

"Come out!"

He came out, moaning and groaning. His wild, wild hair was all limp and damp. Even his knees were wet. Emma felt very sorry for him. She fetched a warm scarf to tie round his aching head, climbed back into bed and cuddled him until they both went to sleep.

"Don't forget we're going to the dentist today," Dad said next morning.

"Monster can go instead of me," Emma said. "He's got toothache."

"Poor old thing!" Dad said. "Why don't we all go? You can tell the dentist about your monster's toothache, and show your monster the ceiling game."

Emma liked the ceiling game. You lay in the dentist's chair and walked your eyes along a road pinned to the ceiling. Past the Sweet Mountain, through Toothache Gate to the Red Apple Orchard, and on to the Toothbrush Forest.

"All right," she said.

But when she went to fetch him, Monster played one of his tricks. He shrank as small as a flea and hopped into Emma's pocket. He wouldn't come out, even in the dentist's room. But he made noises.

"URRRRRRG … OWOWOWOWOWEEEEEEK!"

The dentist was surprised.

"It's Monster," Emma explained. "He's got toothache."

"I've got the very thing for that." The dentist pulled open a drawer. "Pink Monster Toothpaste! Hold the tube while I look at your teeth. I'll fix your monster afterwards."

So Emma held the Pink Monster Toothpaste tube, and her eyes walked along the ceiling road. By the time she reached Toothbrush Forest, the dentist had finished.

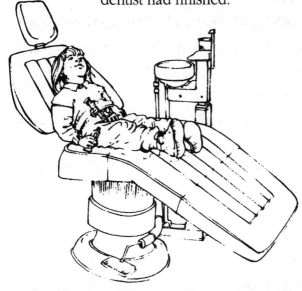

But Monster still hid in her pocket.

"Never mind," said the dentist. "Make him clean his teeth. That will send his toothache away."

Emma took Monster back home and showed him how to clean his teeth properly. Bottom up. Top down. And all round the back.

Then they ran races until it was time for cheese on toast, with a red apple for afters.

ANDREW McANDREW
AND THE
GRANDFATHER CLOCK

by BERNARD MAC LAVERTY
illustrated by DUNCAN SMITH

Andrew McAndrew sat in the front room of his own house. When he was alone Andrew always looked around him and saw as much as he could see. There was a tall wooden clock in the corner with a white face and it ticked very slowly.

Tick! Tick! Tick!

Suddenly the door opened and Andrew's grandad came in. Because he lived nearby he visited them every day.

"Hello, Andrew McAndrew!" he said. "What are you looking at?"

Andrew pointed. His grandad leaned his hand against the clock, which was taller than him.

"This is called a grandfather clock." He knocked on the wood with his knuckle. "Let me show you how it works."

He opened a small door in the clock's tummy and

Andrew saw two big weights on a chain and a shiny thing which swung backwards and forwards, backwards and forwards.

"That's the pendulum. I wind it up like this, by

pulling one of the weights." The chain made a rattling sound.

Andrew said one of his little rhymes.

"Andrew McAndrew, wouldn't it be great,
If you could pull that great big weight."

His grandad said to him, "The clock has to be right because do you know what night it is tonight?" Andrew shook his head. "It's Hogmanay."

"What's that?" asked Andrew.

"This is the last day of one year and at twelve o'clock, when both of the hands are pointing to the ceiling, it will be a new year. New Year's Day and everybody in the town makes a great hullaballoo."

"What's a hullaballoo?" asked Andrew.

"It's noises and cheering. Bells ring and cars toot their horns and ships sound their sirens and trains blow their whistles. Oh, it's the greatest noise you've ever heard."

Andrew sat on the sofa and wished.

"I wish, I wish with all my might
That I could stay up late tonight."

He tried to imagine what all the noises would be like but he couldn't.

"If I wasn't in bed," said Andrew, "could I ring the bell on my wee red bike?"

"Oh, surely, surely, Andrew McAndrew. That would be a great rackety noise."

"Can I stay up?"

His grandad went away to ask Andrew's mum and dad if he could stay up late. Andrew went over to the grandfather clock and opened the wee door and looked inside. He saw the weights and the shiny thing that went backwards and forwards. He pulled one of the weights but just then he heard his grandad coming back. He shut the wee door as quickly as he could.

"I'm afraid," said his grandad, "that everybody says you're too young to stay up."

So Andrew McAndrew had to go to bed at his usual time. He fell asleep thinking of all the excitement and noises he would miss. Then in the dark he woke up. He didn't know what time it was. Whenever he woke up in the dark he always shouted, "I wanna drinka watta!"

His mum came into his room. Andrew asked, "Is it next year yet?"

"No, but it will be soon. I suppose now that you're awake you can come down."

She lifted him and gave him a hug and carried him downstairs in his pyjamas. Everything was bright and shining. All the family were there including Grandad, and they were wearing party hats and drinking drinks. They were all standing round the grandfather clock and both hands were *nearly* pointing to the ceiling. Then Grandad said, "Shhh!"

"What's wrong, Grandad?"

"Shhh! I think the clock has stopped. It can't be – I wound it up today." And they all listened. It was absolutely silent.

"No tick," said Grandad. "Who's been fiddling with this clock?" He looked very cross.

Andrew thought:

"Oh dear, oh dear, I'm to blame,
The clock will never be the same."

Everybody looked very cross. Andrew said, "I'm sorry. I touched the weight."

His grandad said, "Never mind, I can fix it." And he looked at the watch on his wrist and fixed the hands on the grandfather clock and pulled the weight so that the clock started to tick again. Slowly.

Tick! Tick! Tick!

Then the clock made a whirring noise and…

Bong! Bong! Bong!

and everybody shouted, "Happy New Year!" and kissed and hugged one another. Outside the house there was the noise of bells and car horns and ships' sirens and train whistles. Andrew ran into the hallway and rang the bell on his little red bike and everybody laughed. He said to himself:

"I wish, I wish with all my might
That Hogmanay was every night."

ZENOBIA AND THE WILD LIFES

by VIVIAN FRENCH
illustrated by DUNCAN SMITH

It was early in the morning. The sun was floating in little golden sparkles through the gap in the curtains and shining on Zenobia's face. Zenobia opened her eyes and sneezed.

"Oooof," she said, and sat up in bed.

"Um," said Mouse, from under the duvet.

Zenobia looked at the sunshine, and she looked at her rabbit-clock beside her bed. There was something wrong, and she couldn't think what it was. "Mouse," she said, "why isn't today all right?"

Mouse yawned. "Isn't it?"

"No. My tummy feels funny but I don't feel sick."

"What sort of funny?"

Zenobia thought about it.

"It feels as if something's got in there by mistake, and I don't much like it."

81

Mouse scratched his ears. "Maybe you should call Mum."

Zenobia shook her head. "It isn't poorly," she said. "It's just funny. Like when I go to see the dentist."

"Ah." Mouse stopped scratching and sat up. "Are you going to the dentist today?"

"No. Only school."

"Oh," Mouse said.

Mum came into Zenobia's room, and drew back the curtains. "It's a lovely day," she said. "It couldn't be better for an outing. Hop out of bed and whizz downstairs."

Zenobia sat up in bed and stared at Mum. Her eyes grew large and anxious. "Outing?" she squeaked.

"You can't have forgotten," Mum said. "It's today you're all going out for the day."

"I think my tummy remembered," Zenobia said, her voice still squeaky.

Mum looked at Zenobia. "Are you feeling poorly?"

Zenobia swallowed, and felt a lump in her throat. "My throat hurts," she said.

Mum put her hand on Zenobia's forehead to see if it was hot. Then she peered inside her mouth.

"I can't see anything," Mum said. "Does it hurt a lot?"

"It feels all lumpy," Zenobia said. "And my tummy feels even worse."

Mum sat on the edge of the bed and looked at Zenobia. "You'd better stay in bed for a little while longer. I'll fetch you a drink."

Zenobia felt much better at once. "Can I have hot chocolate?" she asked.

"I expect so," Mum said, as she went out.

Zenobia sighed and curled up in bed.

"I think my throat really does hurt a lot," she told Mouse.

"Why?" Mouse asked.

"It isn't why," Zenobia said. "Throats just do or don't hurt."

"Ah," said Mouse.

Mum came back carrying a tray. There was a plate of bread and butter, a banana, an apple and Zenobia's special mug full of hot chocolate.

"See if you can eat a little," Mum said.

Zenobia swallowed again. The lump was smaller. "I might eat a little bit," she said.

"Good." Mum helped Zenobia to sit up, and patted her. "I'll be back in a minute."

Zenobia sipped the chocolate, and nibbled a piece of bread and butter. Then she ate the banana. Then she ate the apple. And then she ate some more of the bread and butter.

"Feeling better?" Mouse asked.

"Shh," said Zenobia. She finished her chocolate with a slurp, and then ate the last piece of bread and butter. "That was nice," she said.

"How's your tummy?"

Zenobia gave Mouse a cross look. "It still feels different."

"It probably feels full," Mouse said.

Zenobia pushed Mouse under the duvet.

Dad put his head round the door. "Not feeling well, chicken?" he asked.

"Not very," Zenobia said sadly. Then she sat up straighter. "Could I have some more bread and butter?"

Dad laughed and took the plate. "That sounds hopeful."

"And some more hot chocolate?"

"Dear, dear." Dad picked up the banana skin and the apple core. "Sure there's nothing else you'd like?"

"Are there any spotty biscuits?"

Dad piled the bits on to the tray. "Hot chocolate, biscuits, and bread and butter. My word, chicken, you'll be too fat to go on your outing."

Zenobia opened her mouth but didn't say anything. Dad went off with the tray.

Mouse made a squeaky noise from under the bedclothes.

"What is it?" Zenobia asked, as she pulled him out.

"I've been wondering," Mouse said.

"Well?" Zenobia asked.

"Why don't you want to go on the class outing?"

Zenobia flopped back on to her pillow. She didn't look at Mouse, but picked at the edge of the duvet with her finger.

"There's going to be wild things," she said in a wobbly voice.

"What?"

Zenobia picked Mouse up and buried her nose in him. She began to cry. "I don't want to see wild things," she snuffled, "they might eat me."

"There can't be any wild things," Mouse said in a smothered voice.

"There are – Mrs Graham said so," Zenobia sobbed. "We're going on a walk to find wild things

86

and bring them back into our classroom so they'll be there for ever and ever." She let out a loud wail.

Mum and Dad hurried in.

"Whatever's the matter, lovey?" Mum asked. "Is your throat worse?"

Zenobia flung herself on Mum's chest. "Don't make me go," she howled, "I don't want to go."

Dad sat down on the bed beside Zenobia. "What's all this about?"

"It's the wild things," Zenobia said in a wet and sniffly voice. She gave a loud sob. "I don't want to collect any wild animals or *anything*."

Mum patted Zenobia's back, and Dad patted her knee.

"There won't be anything scary," Dad said. "Mrs Graham always looks after you – and everyone else in the class."

"But she *said*," Zenobia insisted. "She said we'd go and find wild lifes and bring them back. We're going to have little bottles to put them in – but they might get out!"

Dad pulled a big red hanky out of his pocket. "Here, blow your nose, my poor little dumpling – and I'll explain."

Zenobia blew her nose very hard and sat up on Mum's knee.

"What's a buttercup?" Dad asked.

Zenobia stared at him. "A flower," she said.

"And a daisy?"

Zenobia forgot to snuffle. She smiled. "Another flower. Everybody knows that."

"Well," Dad said, "some people call them wild

flowers – that means they grow without our help. But they don't bite, do they?"

Zenobia giggled. "Flowers don't bite, silly Dad."

"Right. Well, people call worms, tadpoles, spiders and flies wild life – all the little things that you find in the garden and in the park. That's what Mrs Graham means."

"I don't like spiders much," Zenobia said.

"But they don't eat you," Mum said. "And they can't even tickle you if they're safe in a bottle." Zenobia was very quiet for a moment.

Then she looked up.

"Can I have more bread and butter and hot chocolate when I'm dressed?"

Zenobia was ready to go on the outing. She had on her jeans and her anorak, and her packed lunch was in a shoulder bag.

"I'll take you in the car," Dad said. "Just in case a wild thing attacks you in the high street."

Zenobia made a face at him. "I won't be a minute." She flew up the stairs to her room, and came back with Mouse under her arm.

"It's just in case," she said. She looked at Dad out of the corner of her eye. "I mean, even if the wild lifes are very little, I might need a wild Mouse to look after me."

Dad laughed, and went out to the car. Zenobia followed with Mouse.

"Grrrr," said Mouse.

MARY MARY

by SARAH HAYES
illustrated by HELEN CRAIG

There was once a little girl called Mary Mary. Her real name was Mary, but everyone called her Mary Mary because she was so contrary. It didn't matter what you said, Mary Mary always said something different. If you said yes, Mary Mary said no. If you said good, Mary Mary said terrible. If you said it was hot, Mary Mary said it was freezing. She was just plain contrary.

Above the town where Mary Mary lived was a hill, and on top of the hill stood a huge house where a giant lived. The people in the town were terrified of the giant and they ran away whenever they saw him. Not Mary Mary. She wasn't afraid of any old giant, or so she said. No one believed her.

But one day Mary Mary set off to visit the giant. The other children followed her as far as they dared.

Mary Mary climbed right up to the top of the hill and on to the giant's huge doorstep. Then she began to bounce her ball against the door.

The great door opened suddenly. The other children screamed and ran away. Not Mary Mary. She stayed just where she was on the step.

Then something peculiar happened. An enormous splash of salty water suddenly landed on Mary Mary's head and knocked her clean off the step.

The next thing she knew, Mary Mary was flat on her back, wrapped in a sheet, staring at the ceiling. It seemed a very long way off. Mary Mary sat up and gave a little gasp. She saw that she was sitting in a giant matchbox on a giant table with the giant himself looking right at her. But she wasn't afraid. Well, not really. Not Mary Mary.

The giant spoke in a hoarse voice that sounded as if it hadn't been used much. "You're all right," he said.

"No, I'm not," said Mary Mary. "I ache all over." She climbed out of the box and took a good look at the giant. "Hm," she said, "you are big."

"I'm too big," said the giant.

"No, you're not," said Mary Mary. "You're a giant."

"Everyone's afraid of me," said the giant.

"No, they aren't," said Mary Mary. "I'm not."

The giant didn't believe her. Tears welled up in his eyes and began to roll down his cheeks. Mary Mary remembered the great salty splash which had knocked her off the step.

"And I'm a mess," sniffed the giant.

Mary Mary started to say, "No, you're not," but then she stopped. The giant was right. He was a mess. A dreadful mess. And so was his house. Mary Mary dragged her sheet across to where the giant was sitting and dried his tears as best she could.

"You really aren't afraid of me?" said the giant.

"No, I'm not," said Mary Mary.

"And I'm really not too big?"

"Not for a giant," said Mary Mary.

"But I am a mess?"

"Yes," agreed Mary Mary. "You're definitely a mess." She felt very odd. Not contrary at all. "What you need," she said firmly, "is managing."

94

And for the rest of the day Mary Mary managed the giant. First they did house managing: they tidied and washed and polished and sewed and glued and sorted. Then they did garden managing, and raked and swept and clipped and weeded.

By that time they were both filthy, so the giant heated some water for baths. Mary Mary had her bath in a tea-cup. Then she and the giant sat down with pens and paper to do a last bit of managing.

Just before sunset Mary Mary climbed into the giant's waistcoat pocket, and the giant took her home. In his hand the giant held a large envelope.

When the people in the town heard the giant's footsteps come whumping down the hill, they all ran into their houses and locked their doors. The Mayor hid under his bed. Then the whumps went back up the hill, and there was silence. People began to creep back on to the streets. Then a shout went up – "It's Mary Mary, and she's safe!" Everyone began to crowd into the market square. There was Mary Mary, standing beside a huge envelope. And she was smiling.

The Mayor heard the noise of people shouting, and came out from under his bed. He marched out on to the square.

"So you managed to escape from the giant," he said.

"No, I didn't," said Mary Mary, "he brought me home."

"But he eats children for breakfast," said the Mayor.

"No, he doesn't," said Mary Mary, "he eats bread and jam for breakfast like everyone else, only bigger." But no one believed her. They thought she was just being contrary.

"Read the letter," said Mary Mary.

It took a few minutes to open the envelope and a few more minutes to unfold the paper and read the writing.

This is what it said:

GRAND OPENING
TOMORROW

GIANT PLAYGROUND
HILL HOUSE

Wear old clothes

(Manager: MARY
MARY)

The children forgot all about being frightened of the giant, and began to look very excited.

"You can't go," said the Mayor.

"Yes, they can," said Mary Mary.

"Of course we can," said the children.

Very early next morning the children streamed up the hill towards the giant's house. The Mayor and the grown-ups followed as fast as they could. But when they arrived, wheezing and panting, at the top of the hill, the children were nowhere to be seen. The Mayor and the grown-ups rushed through the giant's open door, through the house and into the garden at the back. Then they stopped.

At first all they could see was children. Children sliding, children jumping, children swinging, children bouncing, children climbing. And then the grown-ups realized that underneath all the sliding, jumping, swinging, bouncing, climbing children lay the giant. Mary Mary was managing things from the top of a tall ladder.

The Mayor marched up. "This playground is ridiculous," he said.

"No, it isn't," said Mary Mary quietly.

"This playground is dangerous," said the Mayor.

"No, it isn't," shouted the children.

"This playground is impossible," said the Mayor.

"No, it isn't," shouted Mary Mary, the children, and the grown-ups all together.

"Then I suppose I must declare this playground open," said the Mayor.

"Yes," said Mary Mary.

At the end of the day everyone walked back down the hill, chatting and laughing. Mary Mary stayed behind to talk to the giant.

"You did it!" said Mary Mary.

"No, I didn't," said the giant. "We did it together."

"Yes," said Mary Mary, "I believe we did."

And from that day on Mary Mary was never contrary again. Well, almost never.

CARRIE CLIMBS
A MOUNTAIN

by JUNE CREBBIN
illustrated by THELMA LAMBERT

On Saturday, Carrie was going to climb a mountain.

"Will there be snow?" she asked one morning at breakfast. "Will we need ice-picks?"

"No," said Dad. "It's a green mountain. Covered in grass. We wouldn't be able to climb it if there was snow."

Carrie was disappointed. They weren't going to climb a mountain after all.

"It's just a hill," she told Bear later. "Covered in grass. Mountains have snow."

Bear looked at her.

"I know," said Carrie. "Hills are better than nothing." She fetched her red woollen hat from the cupboard under the stairs, and a scarf and a pair of gloves. She fetched her *Big Book of Maps* from the living-room. It would be useful to know exactly where they were.

She collected an apple and a banana from the fruit bowl and some newspapers from the kitchen. Newspapers could make a warm blanket.

She would need a flag. She went to the cupboard under the stairs and searched among the buckets and balls and spades for the sandcastle flag. But it had gone missing. So she found a thin stick and a large sheet of white paper to make her own.

All this she took upstairs and packed into her rucksack. There almost wasn't room for Bear.

"That won't do," said Carrie. "Your ears are sticking out. You need a hat. It'll be cold up there."

She borrowed one of her sister Amy's woollen hats. It was a bit big. It almost covered Bear's face. She pulled it up so that he could see.

Every day, Carrie packed and repacked her rucksack. On Thursday, she added a ball of gardening string and a bar of chocolate. She drew and coloured the flag carefully, a range of mountains covered in snow. She coloured it so well, she decided not to take it.

Bear looked at her from the bed. "You're right," said Carrie. "A torch. Good idea, Bear. Torches are always useful."

By bedtime on Friday, Carrie was ready. At the last minute she had eaten the banana but she still had the apple and the chocolate, and Mum was going to give her a packet of sandwiches as well.

At last, she climbed into bed. "Don't get too excited," she told Bear as she snuggled down. "Remember, it's just a hill."

But she dreamed of a high white mountain, covered in snow, sparkling in winter sunshine.

On Saturday, everyone was up early and dressed in their warmest clothes. The car journey took a long time. Amy slept most of the way. But Carrie kept her eyes peeled for the first sign of mountain country, just as Dad suggested.

She saw an early-morning milkman and a dog crossing at the traffic lights. She watched houses slipping by, and fields and rivers. And then hills. Hills on every side, rising up into the dark sky.

"Are we there?" said Carrie.

"Almost," said Mum. "Keep watching!" Then she said to Dad, "The sky is full of it."

"Full of what?" said Carrie.

"Snow," said Mum.

"It *is* snowing!" cried Carrie. "Look!"

Large flakes of snow were tumbling out of the sky as if they hadn't a minute to lose. This was mountain country all right, Carrie told Bear. She held him up so that he could see. They were going to climb a white mountain after all.

And then she remembered. "We won't be able to climb the mountain in the snow," she said.

"It may not be much," said Dad. "It may not settle."

But when they pulled into a village half an hour later, the ground was covered in white.

"What about our climb?" said Carrie. They were all standing by the car, looking at the sky.

"Let's give it a try," said Dad. "The snow seems to have stopped. The first part is along the river and then the path goes up through a wood."

"Which mountain is ours?" said Carrie, taking her *Big Book of Maps* from her rucksack. "We'll need to know the way."

"We won't need your *Big Book* today," said Dad. "There'll be yellow arrows pointing the way. You'll have to look out for them."

Carrie put the *Book of Maps* away.

She pulled on her walking boots. She sat Bear at

the top of her rucksack and lifted it on to her back. Mum lifted Amy into the carrier on Dad's back and all of them set off.

Soon they were leaving the houses behind and Carrie remembered to look for the first arrow. "Where will it be?" she said.

"Could be on a wall, or a tree," suggested Dad.

"Or a gate," said Carrie, running ahead. "Found it!"

Above the gate a signpost with a yellow arrow pointed across a field.

Now Carrie could see their mountain. It was huge. It rose clear up into the sky.

"It's bigger than a house," said Carrie.

"It's bigger than ten houses!" said Dad.

The path across the field led to another gate and another arrow. Carrie was there first. "I can see the river!" she called.

It was fun walking beside the river. The air was crisp and clear. The water was high, rushing and bubbling along over rocks, over stones. She hopped and jumped. She skipped and ran.

"I'm going to climb a high white mountain!" she sang.

"You are if the path's not too slippery," warned Mum.

Where the river curved was a bridge. "Can I cross?" said Carrie. It was a wooden bridge, a plank for your feet and rails at each side to hold on to.

"You can," said Mum. "But we think you'll want to cross further on."

"Why?" said Carrie. She wanted to cross by the bridge. She wanted to stand in the middle and watch the water rushing beneath. "Is there another bridge?" she said.

"Not exactly," said Dad.

"Then I'll just go across this one and come back," said Carrie. "Otherwise I'll miss it."

She started to walk across. She imagined a group of fierce bandits coming towards her. She grasped an imaginary stick and fought them off. "Out of my way!" she cried. "Let me pass!"

Gaining the opposite bank, she saw that Mum and Dad had begun walking on.

"Wait for me!" she yelled. She ran back across the bridge to catch them up.

"Did you win?" said Dad.

"Yes," said Carrie. "Not one of them could stand against my mighty strength."

"I thought so," said Dad.

"Here's your next challenge," said Mum.

Carrie looked ahead. A signpost with a yellow arrow pointed across the river but there was no bridge.

"How do we cross?" she said.

"See those rocks?" said Dad.

"Like huge stones," said Mum.

"Going right across the river," said Dad. "They're stepping-stones. They bridge the river."

"You *step* across the river," said Mum.

"Yahoo!" said Carrie, running ahead. But when she arrived at the stepping-stones, she changed her mind. The stones were huge, as Mum had said, and they looked fairly close together, but between them rushed the river. The river actually rushed over one of the middle ones. And there was nothing to hold on to.

"Who's going first?" said Dad.

"Not me," said Carrie. "It looks dangerous. Couldn't we rope ourselves together? I've brought some very thick string." She took off her rucksack to find it. But Dad shook his head.

"You'll be fine," he said. "Just take your time. Amy and I'll go first. Then you, then Mum."

Carrie put her rucksack back on.

Dad set off. Carrie watched him reach the middle.

"I'll be right behind you," said Mum.

Carrie set off. She stepped on to the first stone and stopped. She took a deep breath and stepped on to the next one. She kept her eyes on the top of each stone and not on the river. She stepped on to the next and the next until she was standing on the same stone as Dad. "Well done," he said.

"This is fun," said Carrie.

"The next one is underwater," said Dad. "But only

a little. You need to step on and off fairly quickly. But not in a hurry. Do exactly what I do."

Carrie did. "Good," said Dad as she joined him. "Here comes Mum."

"It's follow-my-leader!" said Carrie. She paused for a moment to look at the river. This was better than the bridge. The water swirling by was much closer. I'm standing in the middle of the river, she thought. And when she reached the opposite bank, she said, "I liked that."

"We thought you might," said Mum.

"But when are we going to climb the mountain?" said Carrie.

"Now," said Dad. "As soon as we enter the wood. At first the path takes us up through trees."

Carrie picked up the trail again in the wood. It was quiet now, after the rushing river. Not much snow had fallen beneath the trees, though once, where the trees thinned out a little, she said, "It's raining on my nose!"

"It's snowing again," said Dad. "I think it's been snowing for some time but we're sheltered in here."

The path was clear, well-marked, winding on and up. Always up. Sometimes Carrie stopped to look ahead and give her legs a rest. They all stopped for lunch.

"This looks a good place," said Dad.

Next to the path was a rocky outcrop. A pile of rocks fallen higgledy-piggledy made good seats and good resting places for feet and backs.

Mum lifted Amy out of the carrier. Dad spread their waterproofs on a flattish slab of rock but Carrie climbed up a little way. She lifted Bear out of the rucksack and sat him in a hollow next to her.

Amy was crying. "Is she cold?" said Carrie. "Look, I've brought some newspapers. They would make a warm blanket."

"I think she's more thirsty than cold," said Mum. "She'll be fine when she's had a drink and something to eat."

Carrie stopped tugging at the newspapers, which she'd been trying to pull out of the rucksack. She found her packet of sandwiches instead.

"Cheese or meat?" she asked Bear. "Oh," she said, "looks like egg. Never mind, we both like egg. Egg and cress." After the sandwiches, she found the chocolate and the apple and then she climbed down to Mum to have a drink.

Amy was pleased to see her. She was sitting between Mum and Dad, playing with the car keys. She jingled them at Carrie. She loved to hear their jingly-jangly noise. But when Carrie began her climb back up again, Amy started to follow.

"No, Amy," said Mum, grabbing her from behind. "Climbing is for big girls."

Amy howled. She flailed the air with her fists. The keys, loosed from her grasp, skidded across the rock and disappeared.

Amy yelled. Mum tried to soothe her. Dad tried to reach the keys. Carrie, who had seen it all, watched.

"It's no good," said Dad, kneeling beside the crack where the keys had fallen. "I can get my hand into the crack. I think I can feel them. But I can't see them. It's so dark in there."

"Can't you just lift them out?" said Mum.

She held Amy, sobbing, against her shoulder, rocking her backwards and forwards.

"I'm worried I'll knock them further away," said Dad. "If only I could see them."

"Just a minute," said Carrie. Quickly she climbed up the rocks and returned with her rucksack. She dived her hand inside it. "I've brought a torch," she said, fishing it out.

"You've come properly equipped," said Dad. "Shine it into the crack, please." Carrie did. But Dad's hand was too big. It filled the crack, shutting off the light from the torch.

"You try," he said to Carrie. "Your hand won't take up so much room. I'll shine the torch. Can you see them?"

"Yes," said Carrie, leaning over. "They're on a sort of ledge." She reached inside, grasped the keys…

"Careful," said Dad. "Don't drop them…" Out came the keys, dangling from Carrie's fingers.

"Well done," said Dad, giving her a big hug. He put the keys safely in his pocket. "I think it's time we moved on."

Carrie fetched Bear. Mum lifted Amy, now asleep, into the carrier.

"Are we still going up the mountain?" said Carrie anxiously.

"We are," said Dad and on they went, the path winding ever on and up.

"Not far now," said Dad. "Best foot forward." And just as Carrie was thinking she hadn't got a best foot, both her feet were quite worn out, they came out of the wood into the open. Carrie blinked in the bright light. The snow had stopped. The sun had come out. The top of the mountain was in sight.

Dad went ahead to test the path. "It's fine," he

said. "It's steep but it's slushy more than slippery.
Who's going first?"

"I will," said Carrie, her tiredness suddenly
forgotten. Up and up she climbed, slipping a little
now and then but picking herself up, keeping her
eyes on the path in front of her, the sun warm on her
back as she climbed.

And then she was there. With Mum and Dad and Amy beside her, Carrie stood on top of the mountain.

Fields stretched into the distance on every side. Farms dotted the hillsides. Far below, in the village where they had started their climb, the golden cockerel on top of the church spire glinted in the sun.

Carrie felt as if the whole world was spread out before her. There was the river and the bridge, the stepping-stones, the wood and the steep path winding up the last bit of the mountain – a high white mountain sparkling in winter sunshine.

"We didn't need the ball of string," said Carrie that night at bedtime, "or the newspapers or my *Big Book of Maps*."

Bear looked at her.

"But the torch came in useful," she said as she snuggled down in bed. "Good idea, Bear."

TOD AND THE BIRTHDAY PRESENT

by PHILIPPA PEARCE
illustrated by ADRIANO GON

Tod had had a birthday, with birthday cards and birthday presents, and a party with a birthday cake with candles, and party games afterwards.

"What a birthday!" said his father at the end of the day. He was putting Tod to bed, while Tod's mother finished the clearing up downstairs. Tod was in the bath and his father was washing his back for him. "And remember, Tod," said his father, "another birthday very soon!"

"No," said Tod. "I only have one birthday a year, that's all. I know that; and you're just being silly."

"Not your birthday," his father said. "It's your mum who'll be having the birthday."

"Oh," said Tod. He took the sponge from his

father and washed his knees while he thought. "Are you giving her a birthday present?"

"Of course," said his father. "I've bought it already. It's a silk scarf of the colours she likes. There's a lot of blue in it to go with the colour of her eyes."

"Is Granny giving her a present?"

"Yes, a pair of warm gloves."

Tod stood up in the bath. He was quite clean by now. He said, "I want to give her something special. I'll buy her that helicopter in the toy shop window."

"Do you think she'd really like that?"

"I would. That helicopter would be my best thing."

"She's different, Tod."

Tod thought, while his father towelled him dry.

"All right, then. Not the helicopter," he said. "But I want to give her something really, really special. I'll have to think."

"You do that," said his father. "And remember, Tod: most of all she'd like to be given something you've made for her."

"I'll remember," said Tod.

All the next day, on and off, Tod thought, and

then he asked his father, "Could you teach me how to knit?"

"I think so," said his father. "But why?"

"I could knit something for her birthday present. A little mat in blue wool, to go with the colour of her eyes."

So Tod's father looked out some blue wool in the wool bag, and a pair of knitting-needles, and he began to teach Tod to knit. It was very difficult.

In the middle of Tod's lesson, his mother walked into the room. She asked at once, "What are you two doing with my knitting-needles? And isn't that my wool?"

"Yes," said Tod's father. "But it's all right. I'm just teaching Tod to knit. He needs to knit something special."

At that Tod threw the knitting-needles and the wool down on the floor and shouted at his father, "Now you've spoilt everything! It won't be a surprise!"

His father began to apologize; and his mother said quickly, "Tod, I didn't see properly what you were doing, and I didn't hear properly what was said. I don't know anything."

"Yes, you do," said Tod. "You're just pretending not to know. But I know you know, and you know I know you know. And it's all ruined!"

Tod burst into tears and rushed out of the house and into the garden. He rushed down to the very bottom of the garden, behind the garden shed, where he often went when he was feeling upset or miserable.

He was a long time coming back, but his father waited for him. At last he appeared, walking quite briskly and looking rather pleased with himself. He said, "I found something special down at the bottom of the garden."

"You've not been in my shed?" said his father.

"No," said Tod. "I was just looking down, feeling cross, when I saw something lying on the earth where you'd been digging."

"Well, what was it?"

"It's in my pocket," said Tod, "and I'm not going to tell you what it is or what I'm going to make with it, because you can't keep a secret. It's going to be my surprise for the birthday."

Tod went upstairs into the bathroom and shut the door.

Then Tod's father heard him washing something in the washbasin. He scrubbed something with the nail-brush, and then he dried something on the bath towel. Then he came out of the bathroom and went into his own bedroom and hid something there.

Then Tod came downstairs and said to his father, "I'll need string."

"There's a ball of string in the kitchen drawer," said his father.

"No," said Tod. "Not ordinary string. Pretty string. Blue string."

"I think we may have to buy some specially in a shop," said Tod's father.

"I have money," said Tod.

The next Saturday Tod and his father went shopping in the nicest shop in town. Tod's father said to the shop lady, "We want to buy some specially pretty string."

"Blue," said Tod.

"I could perhaps be of more assistance," said the shop lady, "if I knew what the string was needed for."

"You'd better have a private talk with my son

about that," said Tod's father. "I'll be at the men's socks counter."

Tod's father went quite a long way off to the men's socks counter. Tod could see him there, and he could see Tod, but he was too far off to hear what Tod was saying.

Tod said to the shop lady, "I'm making a birthday present for my mum. It's to be a surprise, so it has to be kept a secret from my dad, because he's such a chatterbox."

Tod looked over at his father; but his father was looking at men's socks. Tod brought something out of his pocket and showed it to the shop lady.

"Aha!" said she. "Now I understand why you were thinking of pretty string. But wouldn't ribbon be better – narrow velvet ribbon in a pretty colour?"

"Blue," said Tod, "because her eyes are blue. And velvet ribbon would be good."

So the shop lady got out a drawer full of velvet ribbons of different widths and colours. Tod chose the narrowest ribbon of a beautiful blue, and the shop lady advised him of the length he would need. She cut off that length and parcelled it up for him, and he paid for it.

Then he went off to the men's socks counter and told his father that he was ready to go home.

On the way home, Tod said, "All I need now is an empty matchbox for my present to go into."

"Will it be small enough for a matchbox?" Tod's father asked in astonishment.

"I've just said," said Tod.

When they got home, Tod's father couldn't find an empty matchbox, but he did find two boxes only partly full of matches.

Tod saw what must be done. He emptied all the matches from one box into the other, so that one box was full of matches and the other was quite empty.

In the middle of his doing this, Tod's mother walked in. "Whatever are you two doing with the matches?" she asked.

"Just rearranging them in their boxes," said Tod's father; and Tod quietly said to him, "Well done!"

Tod's mother didn't ask any more questions.

That evening Tod stuck white paper all over the empty matchbox. Then he decorated it with pink and blue crayons. He drew a little picture of himself on top with a balloon coming out of his mouth. Inside the balloon he got his father to write:

HAPPY BIRTHDAY!

The next day was the birthday. Everyone was ready for it, and Tod's granny came for the whole day and to spend the night.

At breakfast time, Tod's mother's birthday presents were arranged round her plate. First of all she opened the parcel that had the silk scarf in it.

"It's just what I wanted!" she said to Tod's father. "Thank you!"

Then she opened Tod's granny's parcel with the warm gloves inside.

"Just what I wanted!" she said to Tod's granny. "Thank you!"

Then she came to the matchbox.

"Whatever is this?" she wondered; and Tod's father and his granny both said, "Whatever is it?"

Tod's mother opened the matchbox. "Oh!" she

cried in amazement. She lifted out of the matchbox a narrow blue velvet ribbon with its two ends tied firmly together. Dangling from the ribbon was a small, unusual-shaped stone. The stone was a pretty, light brown with white markings. What made the stone so unusual was a hole that went right through the middle of it. The blue velvet ribbon went through that hole.

"Oh!" said Tod's mother again. "It's to hang round my neck." And she hung it round her neck. "It's a pendant."

"Yes," said Tod. "That's exactly what it is. Not a necklace; a pendant. That's what the shop lady said it would be."

"It's so pretty!" said Tod's mother. "The velvet ribbon –"

"Blue," said Tod. "To go with the colour of your eyes."

"– and the stone is so pretty and so very, very unusual, with a hole right through the middle of it. Wherever did you find such a stone, Tod?"

"Just in the garden," said Tod. "I wasn't even looking for it. But, as soon as I saw it, I thought I could make something really special for your birthday."

"And so you did!" said his mother. "Thank you, Tod! Thank you!"

Tod's mother wore her pendant all day. In the evening, Tod's father was going to take her out for a birthday treat; and, while they were out, Tod's granny would look after him.

Tod was in bed and his granny was just going to read him his bedtime story, when Tod's mother came in to say good night. She was already dressed for going out; she had her coat on, and her birthday scarf and her birthday gloves. As she bent over to kiss Tod, something swung forward from between the folds of the scarf and knocked gently against Tod's face: the pendant.

Tod put up his hand and took the brown and white stone between his fingers.

"Do you really like it ?" he asked.

"Very, very much."

"But you never said it was just what you wanted."

"How could I, Tod? I couldn't have wanted such a thing, because I couldn't possibly have imagined that such a thing existed: a beautiful stone with a hole through it, found in our very own garden and made by you into a pendant, just for me! It still amazes me, and it's one of the loveliest presents I've ever had."

"Good," said Tod.

When Tod heard the front door close behind his mother and father, he said to his granny, "She's having a specially nice birthday, isn't she? And now you can start reading to me, please."

ONE VERY SMALL FOOT

by DICK KING-SMITH
illustrated by DAVID PARKINS

"What animal has got only one foot?" said the children's father. "I bet you can't tell me."

"I can!" said Matthew and Mark with one voice. As well as looking exactly alike, the twins nearly always said exactly the same thing at exactly the same time. Matthew was ten minutes older than Mark, but after that there had never been the slightest difference between them.

"Go on then," said their father. "Tell me. What animal's got only one foot?"

"A chicken standing on one leg!" they said.

"That's silly," said Sophie seriously.

Sophie was four, a couple of years younger than her brothers.

"That's silly," she said. "It would still have a foot on the other leg. Anyway, Daddy, there isn't really an animal that's only got one foot, is there?"

"Yes, there is, Sophie."

"What?"

"A snail. Every snail has a big flat sticky muscle under it that it travels along on. That's called its foot. Next time you see a snail crawling along, pick it up carefully and turn it over, and you'll see. There are loads in the garden."

"Come on! Let's find one!" said Matthew to Mark and Mark to Matthew at the same time.

"Wait for me," said Sophie. But they didn't, so she plodded after them.

When she caught up with the twins, in a far corner of the garden, each was examining the underside of a large snail. Sophie was not surprised to see that the snails were also obviously twins, the same size, the same shape, the same striped greeny-browny colour.

"I know!" said Matthew.

"I know what you're going to say!" said Mark.

"Let's have a snail race!" they said.

"How are you going to tell them apart?" said Sophie.

"I know!" said Mark.

"I know what you're going to say!" said Matthew.

"Fetch us a felt pen, Sophie," they said.

"What are you going to do?" asked Sophie when she came back with a red felt pen.

"Put my initial on my snail," said Mark and Matthew together.

"But you've got the same initial."

The boys looked at each other.

"I know!" they said.

"I know what you're going to say," said Sophie, and she plodded off again. She came back with a blue felt pen.

After a moment, "Ready?" said Matthew, holding up his snail with a big red M on its shell, and at the same instant, "Ready?" said Mark, holding up his snail with a big blue M.

"Wait for me," said Sophie. "I haven't got a snail yet," but already the twins had set their twin snails side by side on the path that ran between the edge of the lawn and the flowerbed. The path was made of

big oval flagstones, and they chose the largest one, perhaps a metre long. The far end of the flagstone was to be the winning-post.

"Ready, steady, go!" they shouted.

Sophie plodded off. "I'll beat them," she said. She was small but very determined.

Behind the first stone she moved, almost as though it had been waiting for her, was a snail. It was as different as possible from Red M and Blue M. It was very little, no bigger than Sophie's middle fingernail, and it was a lovely buttercup yellow.

As she watched, it stretched out its head, poked out its two horns, and began to crawl, very slowly. It had a most intelligent face, Sophie thought. She picked it up carefully, and turned it over.

"What a very small-sized shoe you would take, my dear," she said. "I don't know whether you can win a race but you are very beautiful. You shall be my snail."

"Who won?" she said to Matthew and Mark when she returned.

"They didn't go the right way," they both said.

"But mine went furthest," they both said.

"No, it didn't," they both said.

They picked up their snails and put them side by side once more.

"Wait for me," Sophie said, and she put down the little yellow snail. It looked very small beside the others.

"Just look at Sophie's snail!" hooted the twins, but this time when they shouted "Ready, steady, go!" neither Red M nor Blue M would move. They stayed stubbornly inside their shells and took not the slightest notice of their owners' cries of encouragement.

Sophie's snail plodded off.

It was small but very determined, and Sophie lay on the grass beside the path and watched it putting its best foot forward.

After half an hour, it reached the winning-post.

Sophie jumped up. "Mine's the winner!" she cried, but there was no one to hear.

The twins had become bored with snail-racing at exactly the same time and gone away. Red M and Blue M had gone away too, into the forest of the flowerbed. Only Sophie's snail kept stoutly on, while the straight silvery trail it had left glistened in the sunshine.

Sophie knelt down and carefully put her hand flat in front of the little yellow creature. It crawled solemnly on to it.

"You have such an intelligent look, my dear," said
Sophie.

"What *have* you got in your hand, Sophie?" said her mother at tea time.

"It's Sophie's snail!" chorused Matthew and Mark.

"Put it straight out in the garden," said the children's mother.

"No," said Sophie in a small but determined voice.

Her mother looked at her, sighed, picked up a box of matches, emptied the matches out and gave Sophie the empty box.

"Put it in there till after tea," she said, "and go and wash your hands."

All that evening Sophie played with her snail. When it was bedtime, and she was ready to wash and do her teeth, she put the snail carefully on the flat rim of the washbasin.

Then (as she always did) she filled the basin with warm water right up to the overflow and washed her face and hands. The snail did not move, though it appeared to be watching.

Then (as she always did) she brushed her teeth very hard, making a lot of froth in her mouth and spitting the bubbly blobs of toothpaste out on top of the rather dirty water. She always liked doing this. The toothpaste blobs made strange shapes on the surface of the water, often like a map of the world. Tonight there was a big white Africa at one side of the basin.

Then (as she always did) she pulled the plug out, but as she turned to dry her hands the sleeve of her dressing gown scuffed the rim of the basin. Right into the middle of disappearing Africa fell a small yellow shape, and then the last of the whirlpooling frothing water disappeared down the plug hole, leaving the basin quite empty.

Sophie plodded down the stairs.

"My snail's gone down the plug hole," she said in a very quiet voice.

"You couldn't have kept it, you know," said her father gently. "It would have died anyway without its natural food."

"Next time you find one," said her mother, "just leave it in the garden. There are lots of other snails there, just as nice."

"Not as nice as my snail," said Sophie. She looked so unhappy that for once the twins said different things, in an effort to comfort her.

"'Spect it died quickly," said Matthew.

"Sure to be drowned by now," said Mark.

* * *

Try as she would, Sophie could not stop herself thinking about what happened to you if you went down a plug hole. She lay in bed and thought about the twins washing their hands in the basin and washing their teeth, and then later on Mum and Dad doing the same. All that water would be washing the body of her snail farther and farther away, down the drain into the sewer, down the sewer into the river, down the river into the sea.

When at last she slept, she dreamed that she was walking by the seaside, and there she saw, washed up on the beach, a familiar little yellow shape. But when she ran and picked it up, it had no head, no horns, no foot. It was just an empty snail shell.

Sophie woke early with the feeling that something awful had happened, and then she remembered what it was.

She plodded along to the bathroom and looked over the rim of the washbasin at the round plug hole with its metal grating meant to stop things going down it.

"But you were too small," she said.

Leaning over as far as she could reach, she stared sadly into the black depths of the plug hole. And as she stared, suddenly two little horns poked up

through the grating, and then a head, and then a shell no bigger than her middle fingernail, a shell that was a lovely buttercup yellow.

Very carefully, Sophie reached out and picked up her small determined snail.

Very quietly she plodded down the stairs and opened the back door and went out into the garden and crossed the dewy lawn.

Very gently, at the exact spot she had found it, she put her snail down and watched it slowly move away on its very small foot.

"Goodbye, my dear," said Sophie. "I hope we meet again," and then she sat happily on the wet grass watching, till at last there was nothing more to be seen of Sophie's snail.

Acknowledgements

"Clever Cakes" from *Clever Cakes and Other Stories*
Text © 1991 Michael Rosen   Illustrations © 1991 Caroline Holden

"The Story of Queenie and Treacle" from *Friends Next Door*
Text © 1990 Susan Hill   Illustrations © 1992, 1995 Paul Howard

"Angels on Roller-skates" from *Angels on Roller-skates*
© 1990, 1995 Maggie Harrison

"The Apple Child" from *Under the Moon*
Text © 1993 Vivian French   Illustrations © 1993 Chris Fisher

"Toothache" from *Emma's Monster*
Text © 1992 Marjorie Darke   Illustrations © 1992 Shelagh McNicholas

"Andrew McAndrew and the Grandfather Clock" from *Andrew McAndrew*
Text © 1988 Bernard Mac Laverty   Illustrations © 1988 Duncan Smith

"Zenobia and the Wild Lifes" from *Zenobia and Mouse*
Text © 1990 Vivian French   Illustrations © 1990, 1995 Duncan Smith

Mary Mary
Text © 1990 Sarah Hayes   Illustrations © 1990, 1995 Helen Craig

"Climbing the Mountain" from *Carrie Climbs a Mountain*
Text © 1993 June Crebbin   Illustrations © 1993 Thelma Lambert

"Tod and the Birthday Present" from *Here Comes Tod!*
Text © 1992 Philippa Pearce   Illustrations © 1992 Adriano Gon

"One Very Small Foot" from *Sophie's Snail*
Text © 1988 Fox Busters Ltd   Illustrations © 1994 David Parkins